LUCY MCGEE

DISCARD

A STAR ON TV,
LUCY MCGEE

BY

MARY AMATO

ILLUSTRATED BY

JESSICA MESERVE

HOLIDAY HOUSE NEW YORK

Library of Congress Cataloging-in-Publication Data

Names: Amato, Mary, author. | Meserve, Jessica, illustrator.

Title: A star on TV, Lucy McGee / by Mary Amato ; illustrated by Jessica Meserve.

Description: First edition. | New York : Holiday House, [2020] | Series:

Lucy McGee | Audience: Ages 7-10. | Audience: Grades 4-6. | Summary: "A

chance to be on TV brings out the worst in fourth grader Lucy McGee—and

now her friends want her out of the Songwriting Club!"—Provided by publisher.

Identifiers: LCCN 2020039143 | ISBN 9780823446063 (hardcover)

ISBN 9780823448302 (trade paperback) | ISBN 9780823448845 (ebook)

Subjects: CYAC: Friendship—Fiction. | Clubs—Fiction. | Schools—Fiction.

Television programs—Fiction.

Classification: LCC PZ7.A49165 Sr 2020 | DDC [Fic]—dc23

LC record available at https://lccn.loc.gov/2020039143

ISBN 978-0-8234-4606-3 (hardcover)

ISBN 978-0-8234-4830-2 (paperback)

For Juliet Wade

A STAR ON TV,
LUCY MCGEE

CONTENTS

Chapter One

MY BRAIN IN THE RAIN

I hate wet socks. When it's raining and you can't find your rain boots, you have to be careful walking to school.

Today there were puddles everywhere. By the time I got to the end of my street, I had hopped over seven big ones. Only two blocks more to get to my school. So far so good. My dad was way behind me with Leo and

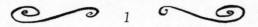

Lily and the big black umbrella. They were walking super slow because my little brother, Leo, had to name every worm he saw on the sidewalk.

Wumpy, Chumpy, Humpy, Dumpy . . . Leo is excellent at names.

I walked ahead with my blue umbrella in one hand and my ukulele in the other. I turned the corner. *Whoa!* Right in front of the sidewalk heading into school was the biggest puddle of all. It was deep and wide and long and muddy.

I crouched down and got all my energy ready. I leaped! I soared! My feet lifted into the air and landed . . . *plop!* Right in the middle.

Disgusting.

I turned back and saw a red umbrella with legs and a ukulele poking out from under it heading for the same puddle. I knew those legs.

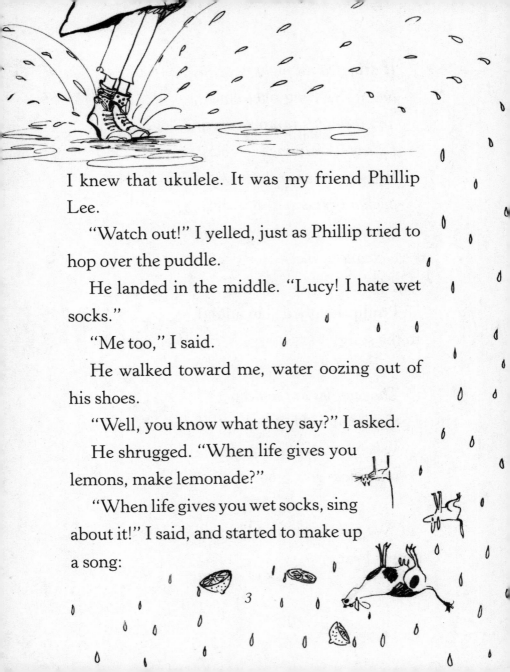

I knew that ukulele. It was my friend Phillip Lee.

"Watch out!" I yelled, just as Phillip tried to hop over the puddle.

He landed in the middle. "Lucy! I hate wet socks."

"Me too," I said.

He walked toward me, water oozing out of his shoes.

"Well, you know what they say?" I asked.

He shrugged. "When life gives you lemons, make lemonade?"

"When life gives you wet socks, sing about it!" I said, and started to make up a song:

It drizzled all night
and it's pouring right now.
You think it's raining cats and dogs?
I'd say it's raining . . . cows!
Before you leave the house,
pack an extra pair of socks,
especially if you have to walk
a couple of blocks.

Phillip laughed. He added
to the song:

The puddles are so deep
they're probably filled with fish.
When you step in a puddle
your shoes go . . . squish.

"We got the rhymes!" I said. "Now it's finish
time." I sang:

4

So pack that extra pair
of socks for your feet.
Your toes will thank you
and think you're sweet.

Phillip tried to clap, which was hard because he was holding his umbrella.

We sang the song again. Another umbrella with legs stopped to listen.

"Great song!" The umbrella lifted up. It was Pablo.

As we walked into the school together, Pablo said, "Hey, I've got an idea. It's my turn to read the weather report on *The Morning Mix*. Teach me the song, and we'll sing it together on the

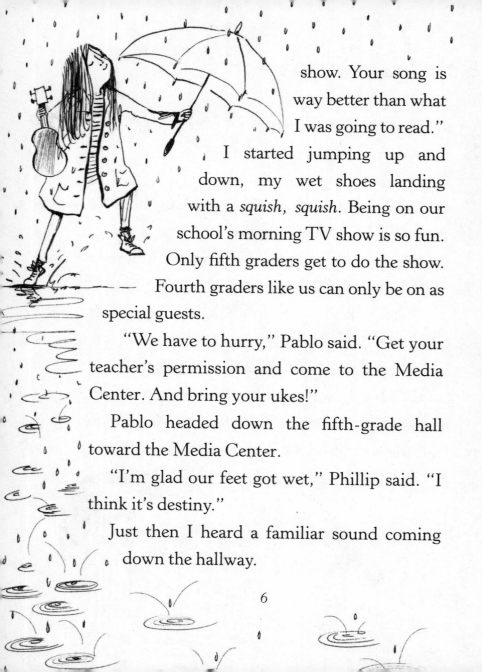

show. Your song is way better than what I was going to read."

I started jumping up and down, my wet shoes landing with a *squish, squish.* Being on our school's morning TV show is so fun. Only fifth graders get to do the show. Fourth graders like us can only be on as special guests.

"We have to hurry," Pablo said. "Get your teacher's permission and come to the Media Center. And bring your ukes!"

Pablo headed down the fifth-grade hall toward the Media Center.

"I'm glad our feet got wet," Phillip said. "I think it's destiny."

Just then I heard a familiar sound coming down the hallway.

6

Clack, clack, clack.

I pulled Phillip behind Mr. Tapper's big rolling garbage bin.

"What are we doing?" Phillip asked.

"Shh! We're hiding."

I crouched down.

"Why?" he whispered, and crouched down next to me.

"Listen . . ."

Clack, clack, clack.

We peeked out. Scarlett Tandy was coming. Scarlett is a friend of ours and she's also in the Songwriting Club, which Phillip started. She can be fun, but she can also be a tornado of trouble. If Scarlett found out what we wanted to do, I was afraid she would make herself the star. I just wanted to keep it simple.

I crossed my fingers and hoped she didn't see us.

7

Chapter Two

WORM SQUIRM

Hiding behind a garbage bin is hard enough. Hiding behind it when you're dripping wet and you have a backpack and a ukulele and an umbrella and you have to sneeze is even worse. I pinched my nose to keep from sneezing and we waited.

Clack, clack, clack. Scarlett's shoes were coming.

Of course Scarlett's shoes didn't go *squish, squish, squish*. Even though she lives next to the school, her parents drive her whenever it rains.

The sound was getting closer and closer and my nose was getting ticklier and ticklier. And then Phillip's eyes got huge. He pointed at my foot. I looked down.

Wriggling around on the tip of my shoe was a worm!

Phillip started to laugh, picked up the worm, and dangled it in front of my face, which made me want to laugh. My laugh and my sneeze came out in one big *"Haha-achoo!"*

Scarlett heard. "What are you two doing back here?"

Phillip looked at me. "What are we doing, Lucy?"

"Nothing. We're just hanging out with our

new friend Wumpy," I said, and held up the worm.

"Ew!" Scarlett yelled as she *clack, clack, clack*ed away. "You guys are disgusting!"

Phillip and I stood up.

"Was that mean of me?" I asked him. "I just think that if Scarlett knows what we're doing, something bad will happen."

He shrugged. "She always wants to be the boss of everything. It's a problem." Then he gave me one of his looks. "But she's going to find out."

"Let's not go to our classroom. Let's just go to the Media Center and do it!" I said. "We're studying weather in science now, Phillip. Mrs. Brock will love our idea. Once she sees us on TV, she'll be so proud of us she won't care!"

Phillip shook his head. "No way. We need permission. Even if it means Scarlett finds out.

Come on or Mrs. Brock will think we're absent.
Bring Wumpy along and we can put her in Mrs.
Brock's ivy plant."

I looked at Phillip. He just didn't understand.
I had to take control, but how? And then a
sneaky idea popped into my head.

"I've got it!" I said. "I know a way to tell
Mrs. Brock what we want to do without Scarlett
finding out! I'll take care of Mrs. Brock. You go
to the Media Center and tell Ms. Dell that I'm
coming."

"What if Mrs. Brock says no?"

"She won't! See you in a minute."

I put Wumpy in my pocket and headed
toward our classroom. When I was outside the
door, I set down my stuff and got out a piece of
paper and a pencil.

Dear Mrs. Brock,

There is an emergency. Phillip and I must sing the weather report on *The Morning Mix*. We will be a little late to class, but it will be worth it. This is our duty.

Your helpful student,

Lucy McGee

I folded up the paper. Then I peeked into the classroom. Everybody was putting stuff in their cubbies.

I slipped the paper under the door and walked as quickly as possible to the Media Center. Mrs. Brock would see the note and be happy that two of her students were being creative and helpful. What could go wrong?

Chapter Three

THE FLOW
OF THE
SHOW

Being on TV sounds fun until the camera is pointed at
your face!

In the Media Center, I stood on one side of Pablo,
and Phillip stood on the other side. We had to be silent
while a fifth grader named Tariq read the news. Then
the camera turned to us.

You know how people say when you're nervous you have butterflies in your stomach? I had a swarm of a thousand butterflies.

"Hi!" Pablo said to the camera. "Today I have some special guests who are going to sing about today's weather with me. Here's Lucy McGee and Phillip Lee."

I couldn't remember how the song went! I panicked. And then I looked at Phillip.

He looked perfectly calm. He started strumming and smiling in his Phillipy way, and I knew I'd be okay. *"It drizzled all night and it's pouring right now."*

I joined in. *"You think it's raining cats and dogs? I'd say it's raining . . . cows!"*

I was going with the flow until I felt another sneeze coming on. I tried and tried to hold it in. But as soon as I sang the last word, I sneezed. At the same time, I pulled a tissue out of my pocket. And when that tissue flew out of my pocket, Wumpy came with it! That worm sailed across the room and landed right on the camera lens!

Oh no! Worm Close-Up!

I froze.

And then everybody in the room burst into laughter and clapped.

"The worms are out on this rainy Tuesday!" Pablo said. "Have a great day. Don't forget to tune in tomorrow for *The Morning Mix*."

Hearing applause is the best sound in the world.

"That was the most creative weather report we have ever had," Ms. Dell said.

I plucked Wumpy from the camera lens and put her back in my palm. She was still wriggling.

"You guys should come back and do more weather reports," Cristina said.

I sang: "*Sun, rain, sleet, snow. We can write a song for every show.*"

Ms. Dell laughed. "You definitely got the rhymes! I'll talk to Mrs. Brock about it at lunchtime. Everybody get to class."

Pablo fist-bumped us, and we collected our stuff and started to walk out.

"Wait!" I stopped. "Can we put Wumpy back outside, Ms. Dell? My brother Leo would divorce me from the family if I let a worm die."

She smiled and opened a big window. "There's a lovely world of mud right here just waiting for a worm like yours."

I plopped Wumpy into the soft mud outside the window. "Thanks for everything, Wumpy!"

Phillip sang: *"Slow, slow squirm the worms gently through the crud.*  *Merrily, merrily, merrily, merrily, life is full of mud."*

On our way back to class, our shoes were going *squish, squish, squish,* but our hearts were going *yay, yay, yay.*

"I bet everybody in our class will clap for us when we walk in," I whispered to Phillip. "This is going to be the best day of our lives."

He nodded and we squished down the hall even quicker.

Excited, we opened the door to our room and then froze.

Everybody was staring at  us, but they didn't look glad to see us. They looked mad!

"Look who's here," Scarlett said. "The Liars' Club."

"Liars?" Phillip looked horrified.

"I asked what you were doing and you said 'nothing.'" Scarlett gave us a mean look.

"That's enough, Scarlett," Mrs. Brock said. "Everybody get to work on your states projects. Lucy and Phillip, stay right there. We need to talk."

My heart wasn't going *yay, yay, yay* anymore. It was going *blump, blump, blump*.

Chapter Four

ME? BAD!
THEM? MAD!

"Lucy! Didn't you get permission?" Phillip whispered. He looked like he wanted to join Wumpy and crawl under a rock.

Just then I saw a folded piece of paper on the floor. As Mrs. Brock walked over to talk to us, I handed it to her. "I left this note for you."

"You left a note on the floor and thought I would read it?" she asked.

"Whenever my brother Leo slips a note under my door, I always read it," I said.

"This is bad," Phillip said.

It was bad. What was I thinking? "It's not Phillip's fault," I said. "It's my infection."

"What?" Mrs. Brock looked confused.

"My dad says I get too excited sometimes and my excitement spreads like an infection and it makes me do things that end up being a problem." I took a breath. "Last night I got excited about dessert and I started hopping in my seat so much I knocked a bowl off the table and it busted. I tried to glue it back together, but that didn't work."

"Let's stick to the subject," Mrs. Brock said.

"Stick to the subject . . . glue . . . get

it?" I said, and smiled at Phillip. Usually he would smile back, but he was looking at his feet. "I'm sorry," I said again.

"Lucy," Mrs. Brock said. "What *should* you have done?"

Even though nobody was talking to her, Scarlett said loudly, "Lucy should have invited our whole Songwriting Club to sing on *The Morning Mix*."

Mrs. Brock told Scarlett to focus on work and then looked at me. "Lucy, I want to hear it from you."

"I should have asked your permission," I said. "I'm sorry."

"*The Morning Mix* isn't a big deal anyway," Scarlett said. "It isn't even real TV. My mom does the real weather on real TV so I know."

"Scarlett Tandy!" Mrs. Brock said. "Do your work and let me handle this. Lucy and Phillip, sit down and get busy. We're not going to talk about this anymore today."

Phillip kept his eyes glued on his feet. He hated getting in trouble more than anything.

I felt terrible. And then I noticed something. Victoria, Mara, and Resa—all the other members of the Songwriting Club who are in our class besides me and Phillip and Scarlett—were staring at me. They all looked mad. Even Resa.

I got out my social studies work. We each had to do research on a different state and write a report about it. My state was Idaho, which is famous for growing potatoes, which is important for everybody who likes potato

chips. I was reading my library book about it when I saw Scarlett pass a note to Victoria. She read it and passed it to Mara. She read it and passed it to Resa.

"Resa," I whispered. "What's in the note?"

Resa acted like she couldn't even hear me. She handed it to Phillip.

That letter was probably about me! I had to see it!

Chapter Five

TIME, TO THINK STINKS

During our break before math, I wrote a note to Phillip.

Dear Phillip,

I am sorry from the bottom and the top and the sides of my heart. Please say it's okay. We could play our ukes

during recess and write another song. And could you please show me that note Scarlett wrote? I'm dying of curiosity.

Your friend forever,

Lucy

P.S. You are the best singer in the world because you don't even get nervous. And I mean it.

He read it, but he didn't even look at me. It was terrible and then it got worse.

When Mrs. Brock said we'd have indoor recess because it was still raining, Phillip and Resa got a word game and sat on the carpet. Scarlett and Victoria and Mara pushed their desks together and played cards. I just sat there like a worm on a sidewalk for a while. First I pretended to read my library book about Idaho. Then I walked over to Phillip and Resa.

"Are you guys ever going to stop being mad at me?" I whispered.

Resa and Phillip looked at each other.

Then Phillip spelled out a sentence on the game board with the square letters of the game.

WE NEED TIME TO THINK

The note Scarlett passed around was sticking out of Phillip's back pocket. I couldn't stand the suspense anymore, so I grabbed it.

"Give it back, Lucy," Phillip said. "You don't want to read it."

I took it over to my cubby and read it.

Dear Songwriting Club (except Lucy),

Lucy was mean for leaving us out. Nobody talk to her. If she tries to talk to you, just pretend you can't hear her.

We can make up our own weather songs. Lots of them. Let's get permission to sing the weather on *The Morning Mix* every day. Without Lucy. Let's not tell her we're doing it. Let's just do it and see how she likes it.

Ha. See ya!

Scarlett

I didn't know what to do. It was the first time in my life that everybody was mad at me at the same time. I couldn't believe that Phillip and Resa were even thinking about going along with Scarlett's idea. I felt like I was going to cry, but I

didn't want to. I was alone in the world. Just me
and my stinking wet socks and my book about
Idaho.

What I really wanted to do was crawl into my cubby and write a song. Unfortunately, our cubbies are not big enough. I took my uke and my songwriting notebook over to the corner of the room. While everybody else was talking and laughing, I sat by the window and wrote a song.

Shout

Rain laughs against the glass.
The clock is ticking loud and fast.
My pencil shouts across the page while
other voices drown me out.

No one can hear me.
No one can hear me.
No one can hear me now.

Why can't I evaporate and rise up from
the ground,
    become a cloud and float to Idaho
    and let my rain come thundering down?
    Then at least someone in Idaho would
hear me falling down.

Hear me falling
Hear me falling
Hear me falling down.

30

I sang my song very softly and it came out good. It's like I have a secret songwriter who lives inside me who keeps me company when I'm feeling lonely—and it's really just me.

Idaho

Chapter Six

WIGGLES AND WRIGGLES

Finally school was over. The rain had stopped, but the sky was gray and the air was cold and had that wormy smell. I hurried home. I wanted to rip off my disgusting wet socks, get a delicious snack, take it up to my bedroom, and eat it in my closet. Delicious food makes me feel better. So does sitting in my closet.

When I'm only halfway upset,
I leave the door open. When
I'm really upset, I close the door
and howl like a wolf, which is
something Leo taught me to do.

As soon as I walked in the front
door, I kicked off my shoes and
peeled off my socks.

Yuck! My feet smelled like dead fish.

My dad poked his head out from the kitchen.
"Hey, Lucy. I'm in here," he said. "Cooking
with worms."

My dad says lots of strange things, but this
was terrible.

"Worms?" I almost started crying. "I had a
very bad day and I was really hoping for a pizza
bagel—"

My dad laughed. "I'm not cooking worms.
I'm cooking mac and cheese."

"Lily and me is being worms!" Leo's voice called out.

I looked under the kitchen table. Leo and Lily were wiggling around on their tummies.

Leo had a huge smile. "Come on, Lucy. Be a worm with us."

Lily took her pacifier out of her mouth and pointed it at me. "Yucy be wom!" she said, which meant Lucy be a worm! She still hasn't figured out all her sounds, but she knows how to be bossy in a very cute way.

"I'm going to my closet," I said. "I had the worst day of my life."

"What happened?" my dad asked.

"I made a big mistake and nobody likes me anymore," I said. "Not Resa, not even Phillip."

"I like you," Leo said.

"Thank you, Leo," I said.

"But I'd like you more if you were a worm," he said.

My dad laughed.

"I don't know if I have the energy to be a worm." I sat on the kitchen floor. "I am being serious."

"Worms is fun. We come out when it rains," Leo said. "We like the rain."

"Wain. Wain. Wain," Lily said, and wriggled onto my lap.

"Try it," Leo said.

"Twy it!" Lily said.

My dad smiled. "It might be just what you need."

I scooched Lily off my lap and got on my tummy.

"Wriggle!" Leo said.

"Wigga!" Lily said.

They started wriggling with their little faces

close to mine. I started wriggling, too, and then we all started giggling.

"Okay. I'm in!" my dad said, and got down on the floor.

We wiggled and wriggled and giggled, and then we heard the front door open.

"I'm home!" my mom's voice called out. "Where is everybody?"

Lily's eyes got huge and she took her pacifier out of her mouth. "Mama wom!" she squealed. My mom came in and joined the pile.

A bad day can get way better if you're lucky enough to belong to a family that's willing to wiggle and wriggle and giggle together.

Chapter Seven

CRUNCH FOR LUNCH

When I woke up, I remembered how mad everybody was at me. It's scary to go to school when everybody is mad at you. It's also sad. They were going to write weather songs today and ask Ms. Dell if they could sing on *The Morning Mix* every day. How was I going to survive?

And then I opened the front door and saw that the weather matched my mood.

"Whoa!" I said.

My family came to look.

"What is it?" Leo asked.

"That's called fog," my mom said. "We don't get it very often here."

"It's like a grayish cloud is sitting on our street," I said. "Isn't it creepy?"

"Is it going to be like this forever?" Leo asked.

"No, the sun will probably burn through it soon," my dad said.

The fog looked exactly how I felt on the inside—like a scary cloud was sitting on my soul.

"It feels like nighttime," Leo said. "I want to walk in it!"

"Me too," Lily said, and ran to put on her rain boots.

"It's Wednesday," my mom said. "Don't forget your uke, Lucy."

Today was Wednesday, which meant Songwriting Club. Usually I love Wednesdays. But nobody was going to want me there. I felt like crying. If I hadn't gotten that sneaky idea to write Mrs. Brock that note, this never would have happened. *I hope I never get another sneaky idea,* I thought. And then a new sneaky idea popped into my head!

I could hand out a surprise to my friends at lunch.

What kind of surprise would *I* like at lunch? Potato chips!

I got two little bags of potato chips. "Mom, can I take these to school to share with my friends, please, please, please? It's a matter of life and death. Phillip and Resa are mad at me and this will win them back."

"Lucy, a good friend doesn't need to be bribed," she said.

"Please?" I asked. "I'll pay you back."

"Okay." My mom smiled. "As long as you're not going to eat them all yourself."

I put the chips in my backpack, got my uke, and headed out. The fog made it extra dramatic. It was the same street as yesterday, but the weather made it look like a suspenseful movie.

The rhythm of my footsteps gave me a beat inside my head. I couldn't help it. A song popped out. I sang it to myself as I walked along.

Life today turned upside down.
Clouds are drooping to the ground.
The sun got scared and stayed in bed.
Are those trees or ghosts ahead?
Grayish mists are deeply creeping.
Is the whole world wet and weeping?

41

Wolves and zombies—did I mention?—
love this weather. Pay attention!
As you walk alone, beware!
The fog can hide what's hiding there.

Suddenly two shapes appeared in front of me on the sidewalk. I screamed.

"It's just us, Lucy," Phillip said. "We heard your song. It's great."

"I didn't even see you!"

Both Phillip and Resa laughed.

"I like the zombie part," Resa said.

I was shocked. "You aren't still mad at me?" I asked.

Phillip shrugged. "I can't really stay mad at anybody who's that good at songwriting."

"Me either," Resa said. "I was going to tell Scarlett today that we shouldn't sing without you. Phillip and I were just talking about it."

"Two wrongs don't make a right," Phillip said.

I started jumping up and down. "Thank you! Thank you! I can teach you my song and we can sing it together."

"Can I make one suggestion?" Phillip asked.

I nodded.

"At the end, instead of singing 'The fog can hide what's *hiding* there,' we could sing a different word," he said. "We could sing 'The fog can hide what's *lurking* there.'"

"I love it! Two heads are better than one," I said.

"That's what zombies say," Phillip said.

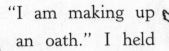 "I am making up an oath." I held

43

up my right hand. "I promise to never get my friends in trouble. I promise to tell the whole Songwriting Club whenever there is a singing opportunity and to include everybody."

"Come on," Resa said. "Let's all go talk to Scarlett."

We walked over to where Victoria, Mara, and Scarlett were in a huddle by the door.

"Scarlett," Resa said. "Lucy has made an oath and she has also written a new song for all of us to sing. All of us."

"One for all and all for the Songwriting Club," Phillip said.

Scarlett looked at me. "Let's hear it, Lucy."

I said the oath and sang the song and looked at them.

"That *is* a good song," Mara said.

"Well, I think the oath should be in writing," Scarlett said.

"An official oath! I like it," Phillip said. "Everybody in the Songwriting Club can sign it."

"Whoever has the best handwriting should write it," Scarlett said.

"You have really pretty handwriting, Scarlett," Victoria said. "Write it with a glitter pen."

Scarlett smiled. "I'll make it perfect."

"After school we'll sign the oath and get permission to all sing on *The Morning Mix* every day!" Phillip said. "We have a rain song and a fog song. We need to have a song for every kind of weather so we're ready for anything."

The whistle blew and everybody headed inside.

Then Phillip stopped and turned around.

Resa and I stopped and looked at him.

"I'm memorizing the fog," he said. "This weather is the best."

The three of us stood and looked at the creepy mist. And then I remembered the chips. "Close your eyes, guys," I said.

I snuck a bag of chips into each of their

backpacks. "A surprise for your lunch from me, Lucy McGee," I said.

"Thanks, Lucy," Phillip said.

Thanks to Idaho, I thought. *For the potatoes. Crunch* for lunch!

The Song Writing Club

Chapter Eight

CAN WE GET ALONG AND WRITE MORE SONGS?

signed mara SAKI Lucy Scarlett
Phillip Lee Pablo Resa Victoria Nathalie

We promise to include everybody in the club
whenever we get the chance to sing.
Unless, of course, we are in the shower.
Then we can sing by ourselves.

After school, everybody in the club raced to Ms. Adamson's room and signed the oath. Me, Phillip, Resa, Scarlett, Victoria, Mara, Pablo, Saki, and Natalie. (Riley used to be in our club, but he's in Chess Club now.) We told Ms. Adamson the plan, and she called Ms. Dell on her cell phone. Ms. Dell said she'd come and talk it through. It was really happening!

"Let's make a list of all the kinds of weather we need songs about," Phillip said, getting out his songwriting notebook.

"Snow," Resa said.

"Sleet," Natalie said.

"What about regular old sunshine?" Pablo said.

"Yes!" Scarlett danced around. "Beautiful sunshine!"

"And thunderstorms," I said. "That's different from just rain."

"And hail," Phillip said. "I love hail. Rocks from the sky!"

"Hurricanes!" Mara said.

"What about when it gets too hot and dry for a long time?" Victoria asked. "There's a name for that, right?"

"Drought!" Phillip said. "Good one."

I sang, "*It hasn't rained. The plants are dying. The rivers and the fields are drying.*"

"*Everybody will be frying,*" Resa sang.

I fist-bumped Resa.

We were on a roll.

"Let's write the sunshine song first," Scarlett said. "I think it's supposed to be sunshiny tomorrow!"

"Let's split into groups and each group can write a song," Phillip said. "Then we'll teach each other our songs. That'll be faster."

"We're going to be famous!" Scarlett said.

"I love being on *The Morning Mix*," Saki said. "This is so fun."

"Me too," Natalie said. "Now we'll get to be on it every day!"

We split into groups and each group went to a different place in the room. I was kind of torn because I thought sunshine was the most common weather and

I wanted to write a song that was probably going to get sung.

But sunshine isn't so dramatic. So I decided to work on the drought song with Resa. The boys were doing snow and hail together. The fifth-grade girls were doing hurricanes. And Scarlett, Victoria, and Mara were working on sunshine.

Just then Ms. Dell walked in and asked us to gather around.

"I love the idea to sing the weather every day on *The Morning Mix*, but I have some bad news," she said. "I talked with Mrs. Brock about it, and we both think that just fifth graders should do the weather. We can't have the whole Songwriting Club perform every day on *The Morning Mix*. It's really a show that the fifth graders are in charge of, and, you know, our TV studio is a small room. Pablo and Natalie and Saki, since you're fifth graders, if you'd like to sing the weather, that would be fine. Fourth graders, you can do it next year."

The room was silent.

"But we just signed an oath to always sing together," Scarlett said.

"I'm sorry," Ms. Dell said. "I'll let you all talk it out. Pablo, Natalie, and Saki, you can let me know tomorrow what you want to do."

She left.

"I'm sorry, guys," Ms. Adamson said. "You were working really well together."

"Mrs. Brock and Ms. Dell are both being mean," Scarlett said.

"They're doing what they think is best," Ms. Adamson said.

We all looked at Pablo and Saki and Natalie. They looked uncomfortable.

"Maybe we could sing the songs and say who wrote them," Saki said.

"But the whole idea was Lucy's," Phillip said.

"Not really," Pablo said. "Lucy wrote the

rain song, but it was my idea to sing on *The Morning Mix*."

Scarlett glanced at me. She didn't say anything with words, but somehow her face was saying that all this was my fault.

"I said sorry a million times!" I said.

"I didn't say anything, Lucy," Scarlett said. "I'm just sad! Everybody's really, really sad."

"Maybe we should have two clubs—one for fifth graders and one for anybody else," Natalie said.

"That would be terrible!" Mara said.

"We were all getting along just a minute ago!" Resa said.

"It was too good to be true," Phillip said sadly.

"Okay, everybody," Ms. Adamson said. "You have two choices. You could all decide that it's okay for Pablo, Saki, and Natalie to sing

the weather, and they
could make sure to say who
wrote the songs. Or you could
agree that nobody sings the weather.
Sleep on it and take a vote tomorrow."

This was not good. If the fourth graders
voted that the fifth graders shouldn't sing, then
the fifth graders would probably be mad at us. It
was like a storm cloud showing up on a perfectly
sunny day.

Chapter Nine

A FLYING SPY?
A SPY GUY?

The next morning I was lucky I found my boots because, unfortunately, it was raining. Again.

A red umbrella with legs was waiting for me by the fence.

"I saw Pablo," Phillip said. "He said we're all meeting by the big clock in the main hallway to take the vote."

Just as we started to go in, we noticed Scarlett, Victoria, and Mara under the shelter by the cafeteria doors where it was dry.

"Guys," Phillip called. "We're meeting inside!"

They turned to look at us.

Scarlett is really good at gymnastics and singing and violin, but she is not good at hiding things. Her face was saying something. This time it was saying: *I've got a secret.*

"We'll be right there!" she said. And then she whispered something to Mara and Victoria.

"What do you think is going on, Phillip?" I asked.

"When it comes to Scarlett, I never know," Phillip said.

Inside, we all gathered together.

"Saki and Natalie and I talked about it," Pablo said. "And we decided that the club is more important than singing on *The Morning Mix*."

Saki smiled. "We'll tell Ms. Dell that we'll just go back to the regular weather. An oath is an oath."

"That is so nice," Resa said.

"Yes!" Phillip said. "We can get back to normal club stuff."

"Okay, see you guys later," Scarlett said quickly, and she pulled Victoria and Mara down the hall.

The rest of us looked at each other.

"Where are you going?" Saki called out.

"We have stuff to do," Scarlett called back.

"What does that even mean?" Phillip called out.

Mara threw us a funny look, and they turned the corner and disappeared.

"Did you see how guilty Mara looked?"

Phillip said. "They're up to something."

"Spy on them," Pablo said, and then we all had to go to class.

The morning went fast, and Mrs. Brock kept us busy. The sun broke through the clouds, so we got to go out at recess.

Immediately Scarlett, Victoria, and Mara ran to the bottom of the playground.

Phillip and Resa and I walked down to see what they were doing, and as soon as they saw us they got quiet.

"Hey," Phillip said.

"Hey," Scarlett said.

"We were just wondering what you were doing," I said. "It looks like you're planning something."

"It's private," Scarlett said.

Mara and Victoria wouldn't even look at us.

Phillip and Resa and I walked back. "They're never going to tell us," Phillip said.

"We have to find out a sneaky way," Resa said.

"I wish we had a drone with a built-in video camera that could fly over them," I said.

"I would seriously love a drone," Phillip said.

Just then Jeremy Bing walked by kicking a ball and an idea popped into my head at the same time.

"Jeremy!" I said.

"Um . . . what?" He stopped and looked at us.

"Don't look at us!" I said. "Just pretend like you're tying your shoe and listen."

He looked at his shoe- lace, which happened to

60

be untied. "That's funny," he said, and bent down to tie it.

"We need a spy guy," I whispered. "We think Scarlett, Victoria, and Mara are planning something mean. If you kick your ball down there and go get it, you can hear what they're saying."

"If I do it what will you give me?" Jeremy asked.

"You got anything?" I asked Phillip and Resa. They shook their heads.

I sighed. "I have potato chips."

"Deal," Jeremy said. He stood up and "accidentally" kicked his soccer ball down the hill. We pretended not to notice.

He came back up a few moments later and

crouched near us and pretended to tie his other shoe.

"They're practicing songs about the weather," he said. "They're going to sing them on Channel Four next Wednesday. Scarlett said her mom was excited about it. Did you guys know Scarlett's mom is Janet Tandy? She does the weather for Channel Four."

"Yes, Jeremy. Everybody knows that," I said. "I can't believe this! Scarlett must have told her mom and then she must have said they could sing."

"On real TV. Without us!" Resa said.

The whistle blew to come in from recess.

"This is big," I said. "This is way worse than anything I did."

"What are we going to do?" Resa asked.

"We need time to think," Phillip said. "For now let's pretend like we don't know."

"Let's each try and think of a way to get back at them," I said. "We'll meet at the fence right before school and decide on the best plan."

"Um . . . don't forget to give me your potato chips," Jeremy said.

This was not going to be a good day.

Chapter Ten

WORMS IN THE SUN?
CALL 911!

Mad and sad often go together. All afternoon I was mad and sad because Scarlett, Victoria, and Mara were stealing our idea and not including us. I know I didn't include them when Phillip and I first sang on *The Morning Mix*, but at least I didn't steal their idea.

After school when I walked in the door, Lily was

crying. She looked funny because she was wearing nothing but her underpants and her big yellow rain boots. My dad was washing the dishes.

"Lily is having a crisis," my dad said. "Leo, too."

A crisis is when you cry about something that your parents are tired of hearing you cry about.

"What's Lily's crisis?"

"She wants to take a bath," he said. "But she won't take off her boots. I told her she has to take off her boots when she takes a bath. Now she's mad at me. I think she's coming down with a cold. She's been grumpy all day."

"Lily," I said. "The sun came out. You can take your boots off."

Lily looked at me and cried harder. Also, her nose was pouring.

My dad sighed and got a tissue.

I was afraid he was going to ask me to wipe Lily's nose. But he said, "Lucy, can you please see if you can help Leo? He's in the backyard." He looked out the window above the sink to the yard. "Tell him I'll come out in a few minutes and we can play soccer."

I was going to say that I was having a crisis, too, but I thought it might throw my dad over the edge.

I walked out the back door. In the yard, Leo was hunched over like a little old man on the concrete path that goes from the house to our back gate.

"Hi, Leo," I said. "What's wrong?"

He looked at me with big sad eyes.

"The worms are drying up. See?" He crouched down and pointed.

I walked over. There on the concrete was a dead worm.

"Worms can't live in the sun," I said. "Sometimes they die before they can get back to the dirt. It happens."

"It didn't die. It's just dry." With his chubby little fingers, Leo carefully picked up the worm and took it over to a muddy spot by the flowers. "Dad won't help me put the worms back, Lucy. He's so mean."

"Dad isn't mean. Sometimes parents get overthrown by us. It's a thing."

I looked at the little hole full of dead worms. "Putting them in

67

the ground isn't going to make them come alive, Leo."

Leo looked at me. "Don't say that!"

I sat down on the path. "Why don't we take a break? We could play soccer."

Leo just joined a team for little kids, and he had a game coming up. I thought he would be excited to practice with me. But he marched over and put his hands on my cheeks and looked at me. He does that when he wants to say something serious, and it is super cute. "Lucy!" he said. "We need to put the worms back. They want to all be together."

I got infected with Leo's kindness. "Sure, Leo." I started walking around, looking for dead worms to rescue. "When you grow up, you'll probably invent tiny helicopter drones to fly around and save worms from drying out," I said. "You're a very nice kid."

"Worms are very nice, too," Leo said.

"I wasn't nice to Scarlett, and now she's being mean to me," I said. "If I'm mean back to her, then she'll just be even meaner back to me. It will be an infection of meanness."

"Be nice to her and maybe she'll be nice to you," Leo said. "Make a playdate with her. I like playdates."

An idea popped into my head. I stopped. "A party. Everybody loves parties. I could have a songwriting party on Saturday and invite the whole Songwriting Club. I'll make invitations and put lots of glitter on them. Scarlett loves glitter."

"Lucy!" Leo called out. "Look!"

In his hand, one little brown worm was wriggling.

69

"You're saving that worm's life, Leo!"

"It's Chumpy," he said as he dropped the worm into the mud.

I felt a song coming on.

Chumpy was so grumpy 'cause he dried out in the sun.

But Leo picked him up and put him in the mud.

Now Chumpy isn't grumpy anymore.

Leo grinned.

Everybody loves a good rhyme.

Chapter Eleven

BE NICE.
GOOD ADVICE?

After saving the lives of worms with Leo, I wanted to plan my party and make my glittery invitations. But things got in the way.

1. Homework.
2. Chores.
3. Dessert.

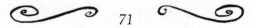

Homework and chores were bad problems. Dessert was a good problem.

My mom wanted to cheer my dad up for having a hard day, so we made brownies and that made us all so happy we played card games the rest of the night.

The next morning when I woke up, I wanted to get dressed and eat fast so I could make my invitations before school. But Lily was in a grumpy mood because she did get a cold, and she spilled milk everywhere and I had to spend time changing my clothes. I packed supplies and hurried to school.

Phillip and Resa were waiting for me by the fence.

"I have a good idea!" I said.

"We've got ideas, too," Phillip said. "Tell her yours, Resa."

Resa jumped right in. "My idea is to give Scarlett's mom's car flat tires on the day they're supposed to go. But I think that's actually illegal. And they could probably just take a bus. Tell her yours, Phillip." She nudged Phillip.

"I've got a great one!" Phillip said. "I think we should all say 'figgy pudding' every time Scarlett says anything to us."

I laughed. "Why?"

"Because it will be annoying to her, and it will make us laugh," he said. "Figgy pudding is just funny."

"What does that have to do with the TV show?" I asked.

"Nothing. What's your idea, Lucy?" Phillip asked. "And most importantly, does it involve a drone?"

"My idea is to have a songwriting party tomorrow," I said. "Everybody in the Songwriting Club is invited!"

"I don't get it," Phillip said. "I thought you wanted to get back at Scarlett."

"I do! My plan is to infect her with niceness," I said. "Remember how much everybody loved the last party I had?"

"That was fun," Resa said.

"In the middle of this party, I'll suggest we all write a new weather song and we can make sure to say nice things about how Scarlett is singing. And then I'll say, 'It would be so cool if we could all sing our weather songs on real TV!'

And you guys can say, 'Yeah, that would be so great.' Because we're being so nice, Scarlett and Victoria and Mara will want to be nice, too. They'll invite us to sing on Channel Four."

"It just might work," Resa said.

"I still like my idea," Phillip said. "Figgy pudding is funny."

"If my idea doesn't work, we can try yours, Phillip," I said.

"Party time!" Resa said.

"I'm going to make invitations with glitter before we have to go in. Want to help?"

"Glitter is brilliant, actually," Phillip said. "Scarlett is crazy about that stuff."

"Maybe we should pretend we don't know about the party," Resa said. "That way Scarlett won't think it's a big plan."

Resa had a point.

The grass was still damp, so I sat on the

bench by the school doors and pulled out all my supplies. Scarlett's invitation first. I folded a piece of paper. Maybe a big glittery star on the front? I could write: *Be a Star at My Party.* She was going to love it.

I took out the bottle of glue and tried to draw the star in glue. But the glue was stuck in the cap. That always happens. Just as I was taking the cap off the glue bottle, the whistle blew to go in. All of a sudden students were rushing by me.

I noticed that Scarlett and Victoria were coming. Uh-oh! I didn't want them to see the invitation before I was finished. I stood up to put away my stuff, but Jeremy Bing raced by at the same time, and we crashed.

The glue bottle went flying out of my hand. *Whoosh!*

It landed on Scarlett's head. *Thump!*

The glue poured into her hair. *Splursh!*

The bottle dropped to the ground. *Thud!*

Scarlett screamed. "Lucy! You did that on purpose!"

Be nice, I told myself.

"I didn't mean it, Scarlett," I said. "I'm so sorry. I was actually making—"

"Look at what you did!" She started to come after me with her hands full of drippy glue.

"Stop that right now!" Mrs. Brock heard us and marched over. "Scarlett and Lucy, you two have been fighting like cats and dogs. Not

another word from either of you until recess, and I mean it. Lucy, put away all that stuff. It's time to go in."

"But I was being ni—"

"I don't want to hear it, Lucy," Mrs. Brock said. "Scarlett, stop touching your hair."

"I'll help you wash it out, Scarlett," Victoria said.

I stuffed everything in my backpack and followed Mrs. Brock in.

Phillip and Resa came along behind me.

"It could have been worse," Phillip whispered. "Scarlett could have gotten slimed with figgy pudding."

Phillip, Resa, and I started laughing.

"It's not funny!" Scarlett screamed from ahead.

But good old Phillip was right. Figgy pudding is just funny.

Chapter Twelve

RHYME TIME

All morning, Mrs. Brock piled on the work. The only way I could prove to Scarlett that I had been trying to do something nice was to give her an invitation. But I didn't even have time to make one.

Finally it was recess. We have a school rule: no backpacks at recess, which meant I couldn't make an

invitation out there. I would have to just say the invitation out loud.

As I was walking out, I had a great idea. I could sing an invitation!

"Everybody in the Songwriting Club meet me outside," I said loudly. "I have an important surprise."

"What are you going to do, throw glue at all of us?" Scarlett asked.

Just be nice, I said to myself. I tried to think up some good rhymes while I was walking out.

When everybody was gathered, I took a breath. And then I sang:

I'm having a party, 'cause parties are nice.
We'll sing and write songs and eat lots of rice.

I just sang that part about rice 'cause it rhymes.

We'll really eat chips and popcorn and limes.

Not whole limes! Just slices mixed into a drink.

It will be a fun party. That's what I think.

"Is it your birthday or something?" Victoria asked.

"No. I just thought it would be fun for all of us."

"It's a really nice idea, Lucy," Resa said.

"You had me at chips," Phillip said. "When should we come?"

"Tomorrow at two o'clock. I'm having it in the afternoon because you'll be done with your gymnastics by then, Scarlett," I said.

"You want me to come?" Scarlett asked.

I nodded. "I want everybody to come."

"What exactly are we going to do?" Victoria asked.

"Hang out and sing the songs we know and maybe write some new ones together."

"Are the fifth graders invited?" Mara asked.

"Yep, everybody in the Songwriting Club."

"I wouldn't miss it," Resa said.

"Parties are fun." Scarlett shrugged. "I guess maybe I could come."

"Me too," Victoria said.

"Me too," Mara said.

So far so good!

Chapter Thirteen

RAIN ON MY BRAIN

When school was dismissed for the day and I walked outside, it was like walking into another world. Dark clouds had moved in and a strong wind was whipping through the trees.

It was very dramatic, like something was about to

happen. I couldn't wait to get home and get ready for tomorrow's party.

And then I remembered something.

I never got permission from my parents to have the party! I had meant to ask last night but everything was crazy.

Hopefully my dad would be in a good mood when I got home. I'd ask right away. What could possibly go wrong?

Leo and Lily were in the living room pretending to kick a pretend soccer ball around. My dad was in the kitchen, making veggie burgers.

"Lucy! Look at me!" Leo said. "I got shin guys on!"

Leo was wearing his soccer uniform and my old soccer shin guards.

"Me too," Lily said, and patted her knee socks.

My dad whispered, "Don't tell her they're just socks."

I laughed.

Everybody was in a good mood. Lily had a runny nose and a cough, but she was happy. A perfect time to explain the party!

"Hey, Dad, I—"

Leo ran over to me. "Lucy, tomorrow I get to wear my cleats for the game. I want to wear them now, but it's too windy to play outside and Dad said I can't wear them inside."

"Me too!" Lily said.

"No, Lily," Leo said. "You're too little to play in the game. It's just me."

Lily turned and looked at my dad and me like she was going to cry.

"Lily, don't worry. You get to come with us," my dad said, and scooped her up. "We're all going to cheer Leo on. It will be fun, right, Lucy?"

I started to have a bad feeling in my stomach. I remembered my dad saying that we'd all go to Leo's first game, but I didn't remember the game was tomorrow.

"Um . . . what time is Leo's game?" I asked.

"Two o'clock."

I looked out the window. That was when the party was supposed to be!

"Tomorrow! Tomorrow!" Leo danced around the room.

"Remember, Leo, if it rains, the game will get canceled," my dad warned.

Canceled? That would be great, I thought. *If it rains, I can do nice things for my mom and dad all morning and then when they're in a really good mood, I'll explain about the party.*

"Is it supposed to rain?" I asked.

"Fifty-fifty chance."

"Lucy, tell the clouds to go away!" Leo said.

"Make up a song for us," my dad said. "Tell the clouds who's boss."

Leo and Lily both started dancing around.

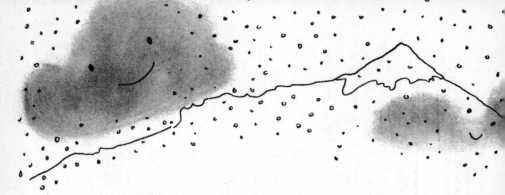

I couldn't tell them that I wanted it to rain.
So I made up a song.

> *Clouds, listen up! You need to go away.*
> *Just think of all the soccer dudes ready*
> *to play.*
>
> *More sun is what we need. Not*
> *a wet mess.*
>
> *Raincoats need a nap. Umbrellas*
> *need a rest.*
>
> *"We're tired of being wet!" shoes and*
> *socks cry.*
>
> *Toes are forgetting what it's like to be*
> *dry.*

So scram for a while. Take a hike. Say
"Bye!"
You're a big wet bully hogging up the
sky.
"You're amazing, Lucy!" my dad said. While
I kept going, he joined in, dancing around with
Leo and Lily.

Go hang out on Mount Everest and turn
into snow.
Adios, amigo. It's time for you to go.
Yeah, plants need the rain, but the
flowers are frowning!
They need the sun, too! The worms are
almost drowning!

Leo stopped dancing. His smile evaporated.
"Lucy, are the worms going to drown?"
"Don't worry!" My dad scooped him up in

a hug. "Worms are really good at taking care of themselves."

My mom walked in and Leo and Lily starting dancing again, and then we had dinner. I just couldn't find the right time to ask either of my parents about the party. As I was falling asleep, I made up another song. I sang it to the clouds very softly.

Clouds, listen up! You need to stay.

I need a game to get canceled so nobody can play.

More rain is what I need. A real wet mess.

Raincoats and umbrellas won't get a rest.

"We're tired of being wet!" shoes and socks cry.

Sorry, little feet, but you can't be dry.

So stick around, clouds. Invite more.
Say "Hi!"

 You might as well have a party in the
sky.

 I was feeling two things at the same time. I really wanted it to not rain so we could all go to Leo's soccer game. And I really wanted it to rain so we could stay home and I could have a party.

Chapter Fourteen

SNEAKY ME, LUCY MCGEE

Some people wake up because of an alarm clock. Some people wake up because they have a cute puppy or a cat that jumps into bed for a snuggle. I woke up because twenty worms were squirming on my face.

Ten of the worms belonged to Leo. Ten belonged to Lily.

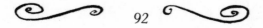

"Get up, Lucy!" Leo said, wriggling his worm-fingers all over my head.

"Up, Yucy!" Lily said.

I sat up and wiped my face. Lily's worm-fingers were especially gross because of her runny nose. They were both wearing the same soccer clothes they were wearing yesterday.

"Dad is sick," Leo said. "Lily was bad and gave him her cold."

"Me no bad!" Lily punched Leo.

"Ouch! That was bad!" Leo said. "Don't be a hitter."

"Stop it," I said, getting out of bed. "Lily, it's not your fault. Don't say that, Leo."

Lily chased Leo out of the room.

I glanced out the window. The sky was blue. There were some clouds, but they were way high in the sky. Definitely a perfect day to play soccer. I didn't know what I was going to do.

"Good morning, sleepy girl!" My mom walked in and gave me a kiss. "Hey, I have a favor to ask. Dad is feeling too sick to go to the game. And I'm worried about Lily's cold getting worse. Would you mind staying home and taking care of Lily so Dad can stay in bed? I'll take Leo to his game."

"That's perfect!" I said. "I didn't want to go to Leo's game because I wanted to have some friends over." I started bouncing with excitement.

"No friends today, Lucy," my mom said.

I stopped. "But I was going to have a songwriting party. We were going to make up songs so we can be on TV. Scarlett's mom—"

"Lucy, no party. Your dad needs a quiet house so he can rest. We can find another day for you to have friends over. I'm making pancakes. Hop into some clothes and come on down." My mom started to leave.

I should tell my mom that I already invited my friends, but I was afraid she wouldn't like that. "Mom . . . ," I said.

She stopped and turned.

I looked out the window at the backyard and a sneaky idea popped into my head. If I took Lily and the snacks outside, and if my friends happened to come over, then we could write songs and eat snacks together in the backyard. It wouldn't be a party. We wouldn't bother my dad at all. In fact, Lily would love it, so that was a huge help. "Mom, since it's nice out, is it okay to take Lily outside this afternoon to play for a little?"

"Sure," my mom said. "Just make sure she's wearing a coat and wipe her nose if it runs."

"Can we bring some snacks outside?"

"Sure, as long as you do all the work. No bothering your dad." She left.

I jumped into my clothes. This would work! On my way down to breakfast, I bumped into my dad.

His hair was a mess. His nose was red. And the pockets of his bathrobe were overflowing with tissues.

"You look terrible!" I said.

He laughed. "Thanks, Lucy. I hear you're going to babysit Lily. Sorry you'll miss the game. But there will be others."

The morning went by really slowly. Leo was so excited, he wanted to wear his cleats inside, and when my mom wouldn't let him, he howled. He was a pain, but it was just because he was so excited. I was glad, then, that it didn't rain. That would have been sad for him.

And then, as the minutes passed, we all kept noticing those fluffy clouds growing bigger and darker. Now I didn't want it to rain!

Finally it was 1:30 p.m. The sun was blocked, but there wasn't any rain. Everything was going to be fine. My mom sat Leo by the front door and put his cleats on.

"Finally!" Leo said. "I been wanting to wear these things all day."

"I told you," my mom said. "Cleats dig into the ground. They're not for indoors."

Leo stood up, suddenly sad. "Oh no! This is terrible!" he howled.

"What?" my mom asked.

He stared at his cleats. "If they dig into the ground, they'll hurt the worms!" He took a big breath and looked at all of us with the saddest face. "I can't play!"

He yanked off his cleats and ran upstairs.

I couldn't believe it.

My friends were coming. Now what?

Chapter Fifteen

SWEET MEET

"I got this, Mom," I said, and ran into Leo and Lily's room. He wasn't there. Then I heard a lonely howl coming from my room. I followed it and opened my closet door.

Leo looked up at me with a sad face. "I want to play, but I can't."

"Leo, it's okay. Worms like cleats."

His eyes got big. "They do?"

"Cleats make holes in the ground, and worms like holes in the ground."

"They do?"

"Sure. Holey ground is better for worms. It brings water down and makes it easier for them to crawl."

Leo jumped up. "If they like holes, I can make a lot of them!" He ran past me and down the stairs, yelling, "Mom! They *like* holes!"

My mom gave me a big hug, and they left.

Whew! That was close.

"Dad, you can go back to sleep," I said. "I'll take Lily outside to play."

He smiled. "I love Leo, but it will be nice to have a quiet house."

After he went upstairs, I got to work. First I put a sign on the front door.

Meet in Backyard

Next I helped Lily put her coat on and stuffed her pockets full of tissues. I got a bag of chips, my songwriting notebook, and my ukulele, and we went out to the backyard. The clouds were huge and dark gray and the sun was blocked, but no rain.

"Hey, Lucy!" Phillip walked through the gate with his ukulele. "I've got a great beginning for a song."

Lily ran over and hugged his legs. "Yup!" she said. That's her nickname for Phillip.

He patted her on the top of her head. "Hi, Lily. Did you know you have stuff running out of your nostrils?"

"That's my job. I'm babysitting," I said, and wiped her nose. "Let's hear your song."

He strummed and sang.

The weather's getting odd.
We're predicting hail.
Little stones of ice will fall.
Collect it in a pail!

Hail can be round or jagged.
Droplets freeze in clouds.
When hail hits your house or car,
it sounds quite loud.

Stay inside today.
Get cozy on your couch.

'Cause playing in a hailstorm
will make your head go "Ouch!"

"That's a great song!" Resa said. She walked through the gate next.

"It's just the first part," Phillip said. "I think it needs more facts."

"Our drought song needs more verses, too," she said.

Before we could work on either, all our other friends came walking through the gate.

"We're doing weather songs!" Phillip said, and held up his uke.

Scarlett and Victoria and Mara looked at each other. And I could tell what they were thinking. They were thinking about the fact that they were going to sing the weather on Wednesday. Without us. Which wasn't fair.

"Scarlett," Resa said. "Weren't you and Victoria and Mara writing a song about sunshine?"

"We haven't finished it," Scarlett said.

"I put in a part about pollen," Mara said. "I have allergies."

"That's good," Phillip said. "We need facts in our weather songs. Sing it. We can all help add a verse."

Scarlett, Victoria, and Mara sang:

The sky is blue. The air is slightly breezy.
The pollen count is low. So you shouldn't
be sneezy.

"That's a great beginning, and you sound really great singing it," I said. I meant it. All three of them are good singers.

"Let's put in something about the temperature," Resa said.

We worked together and wrote more and sang all our songs in a row. Then I wiped Lily's nose, and everybody in the club got excited. Not about Lily's snot. About the songs.

"These are good songs!" Phillip said.

"It would be so cool if we could all sing our

weather songs on a real TV station!" I said, and Victoria and Mara looked at Scarlett.

Scarlett's face turned red.

Mara pulled Scarlett aside and whispered something. Then they came back.

Scarlett said, "Maybe we could all sing on real TV."

My heart started beating like crazy. Phillip and Resa leaned in.

"My mom said we could sing on Channel Four this Wednesday," Scarlett said. "But I'm not sure how many of us."

Saki and Natalie started going crazy. Saki hugged Scarlett. "You would be amazing if you could make that happen, Scarlett."

Scarlett smiled.

"Call her!" Natalie said.

"We can sing her the songs right now," Pablo said.

We all jumped up and gathered around Scarlett. She video-called her mom and we sang and played all our songs in a row. When we were done, we all stared at Scarlett's mom's face on Scarlett's phone.

"What do you think, Mom?" Scarlett asked. "Could we all sing on Wednesday?"

"Those are great songs," Mrs. Tandy said. "Let's have everybody come to the studio. We'll video you singing all the songs and showcase them."

"Woohoo!" We all started cheering.

"Thanks, you won't be sorry!" Phillip said into the phone before Scarlett hung up.

We all danced around.

"One for all and all for the Songwriting Club," I said.

Everybody held up their ukes. "One for all and all for the—"

And then . . . *boooooooom*! The sky rumbled.

We looked up. We'd been so busy singing about the weather, we'd forgotten to pay attention to it. Huge dark clouds had gathered.

Crrrraaaaack! Lightning flashed, and we all jumped. Lily grabbed my hand. Suddenly it began to rain. Everybody started yelling and laughing.

"Let's go inside!" Scarlett shouted, and ran to the back door.

"Wait!" I said.

Too late! Everybody was running into the house!

Chapter Sixteen

INSIDE? TIME TO HIDE!

I picked up Lily and ran into the house.

"Guys!" I whispered. "Shh!"

My friends were all standing in the kitchen, dripping rain all over the floor.

Lily thought it was funny.

Phillip started singing:

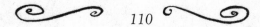

It's raining cats and dogs?
I'd say it's raining . . . cows!

"Please be quiet!" I said.
"Mo cows!" Lily squealed. "Mo cows!"
"Shh!" I said.
But everybody thought she was cute and started dancing around with her singing.

It's raining cats and dogs?
I'd say it's raining . . . cows!

"Guys!" I waved my arms up and down to get everybody's attention. "Please be quiet!"
Everybody stopped and looked at me.
"My dad is sleeping upstairs, and he doesn't exactly know you're here."
"Will he be mad?" Mara whispered.
I nodded.

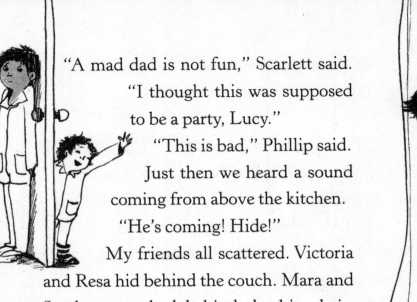

"A mad dad is not fun," Scarlett said. "I thought this was supposed to be a party, Lucy."

"This is bad," Phillip said.

Just then we heard a sound coming from above the kitchen.

"He's coming! Hide!"

My friends all scattered. Victoria and Resa hid behind the couch. Mara and Scarlett crouched behind the big chair. Pablo hid behind the curtains. Natalie and Saki crawled under the kitchen table. And Phillip hid in the bathroom by the front door.

"Hide! Hide!" Lily said, and clapped her hands. Lily loves to play hide-and-seek.

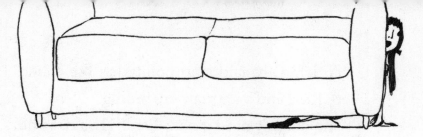

My dad walked into the room. He was in his
bathrobe and looked like he was half asleep.

"Hey, Lucy," he said. "I thought I heard
thunder."

I stood frozen in the kitchen. Nobody
moved. "Yeah," I said. "It started to
rain."

Lily laughed and ran around to peek
behind the big chair.

I tried to pick her up, but she kept
running and laughing.

"You're doing a great job babysitting,
Lucy," my dad said. He walked to the
fridge and poured himself a big glass of
ice water. "Lily, don't you want to take
a nap?"

"Hide!" Lily said, and pointed at the couch where Resa and Victoria were hiding.

"She doesn't need a nap, Dad!" I said. "She wants to play hide-and-seek."

Lily ran and pointed to the bathroom door where Phillip was hiding. "Yup!" she said. "Yup!"

I grabbed her stuffed puppy on the couch and pretended it was barking. *"Yip! Yip! Yup! Yup!* Right, Lily? That's what the puppy says!" I smiled at my dad. "We're playing all kinds of games."

Lily tried to open the bathroom door. "Yup!"

I could see Mara and Scarlett behind the chair. Their eyes were huge.

"Thanks, Lucy," my dad said. "Call me if you need me." He walked out of the room.

As soon as we heard his footsteps on the stairs, Natalie and Saki poked their heads out from under the kitchen table.

"That was close," I whispered. "Everybody has to go!"

Just as all my friends were creeping out of their hiding places, I heard the car pull into the driveway. Oh no! Now my mom was home!

Chapter Seventeen

HIDING PLACE RACE

"Lucy," my dad called. "Sounds like Mom is home."
My dad's footsteps hit the stairs again.

Everybody ran back to their hiding places, and Lily
started clapping again. "Hide! Hide!"

My dad walked into the living room with his big glass
of water. "They must have gotten rained out."

He was just about to open the front door when Leo burst in, dripping wet.

He almost knocked my dad's water out of the glass.

"Gotta go!" Leo said, and ran straight to the bathroom.

"Wait!" I started to say. But he opened the bathroom door, saw Phillip, screamed, and turned around. This time, he did knock the water out of my dad's glass.

The water flew over the chair and splashed Scarlett and Mara. They screamed and jumped up.

My dad was so surprised he fell back on the couch, and that made Victoria and Resa scream and pop up like prairie dogs.

Leo screamed again and ran for the front door, bumping against Pablo, who was hiding behind the curtain. Freaking out, Leo raced toward the kitchen, saw Saki and Natalie under the kitchen table, and screamed even louder.

Just then my mom walked in holding the sign about meeting in the backyard, which I had forgotten to take off the front door. "What on earth is going on?"

My dad looked at all my friends. "I have no idea," he said. "A second ago, none of these kids were here."

Leo started crying and staring at

his shorts. He had gotten so surprised, he wet his pants.

"Oh no!" My mom scooped him up and carried him into the bathroom.

I had a realization. Sometimes sneaky ideas can be good. Like putting potato chips in your friends' lunches. And sometimes sneaky ideas can be bad. Like not asking permission to have friends come over. I got so excited about my sneaky ideas, I didn't stop to think which ones were good and which ones were bad.

"Lucy, what's going on?" my dad asked.

"I invited the Songwriting Club over for a party, but I forgot to ask you and Mom."

"This is very bad," Phillip said.

I went on. "And then I was going to tell you, but it kept getting closer and closer. And then I thought if we were outside, it wouldn't really be a party."

"It wasn't a party at all," Scarlett said. "We didn't even eat anything."

My mom came out of the bathroom with Leo. "I'm going to call all the parents. Lucy, go to your room."

Embarrassed, I turned around and ran upstairs. I sat in my closet for a few minutes, crying. I sort of wanted a drone so that I could fly it down and spy on them, but I sort of didn't want to know what they were saying. I could hear cars come and go, so I knew my friends were all getting picked up.

When I heard my dad's footsteps on the stairs, I climbed into my bed and pulled the covers over my head.

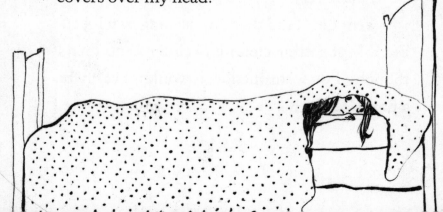

"Lucy, you need to clean up downstairs and then you need to write a letter of apology for every family. When those parents said yes to the party, they thought adults would be in charge. But I was asleep and your mom was gone."

"I'm sorry, but—"

"No buts," my dad said.

"I didn't think it would rain, Dad! We were outside most of the time. We didn't even have snacks. We didn't even make a mess—"

"Lucy! You and your friends tracked dirt and mud in. You need to mop the kitchen and vacuum the living room."

"If I do all that, can I sing with the club on—"

"Lucy, you need to come home every day after school this week. No special activities!

And I don't want to hear a peep out of you." He
pulled off my blanket. "You can start with the
living room. You know where the vacuum is."

I headed downstairs, his words ringing in my
ears. No special activities? I couldn't believe it.
Now everybody would be on TV except me.
Bad, bad Lucy McGee.

Chapter Eighteen

BAD DAY, GO AWAY

When something terrible happens to you, even if you caused it by making a huge mistake, what you really want is for everyone in the world to feel sorry for you. But that wasn't happening.

My mom was on the couch with Leo and Lily, reading a book. She didn't care about how sad I felt.

All she cared about was getting the house clean. "Get to work, Lucy," she said.

I turned on the vacuum, and an idea popped into my head. Instead of spending time mopping and vacuuming, I should spend time inventing hover shoes for the whole family. If our shoes never touched the ground outside, the floors inside wouldn't get dirty!

I turned off the vacuum, grabbed a piece of paper, made a drawing of hover shoes, and showed it to my mom. "I could invent these," I said. "Think about it. No more dirt on the floor."

My mom looked at the drawing. "Nice try, Lucy. Get cracking."

"Get cracking" is what my mom says when she wants me to do something I don't want to do.

When I finished cleaning, my mom put a stack of papers and a pencil on

AIR

FLOOR

the kitchen table and told me to get to work. I had to write my apology letters.

I sat down and started writing.

Dear Phillip's Parents,

I did a bad thing and invited the Songwriting Club over for a party. You trusted my dad and mom to be there. But my dad was upstairs snoring and my mom was out trying to have a good time.

Phillip didn't know, so don't be mad at him. You don't really have to be mad at me, either, because my parents are already mad and there's only so much mad a person can take.

When you think of me, please do not picture a criminal. Picture a girl who made a mistake and who is going to spend the rest of her life crying in a closet. I really am sorry.

Severely yours,

Lucy

Whew! It took a long time to write that letter and I had eight more to write! If I wrote that much for each person, I'd be old by the time I finished.

I picked up another piece of paper.

Dear Resa's Parents,

Sorry for the illegal party. You are grown-ups, and you can do whatever you want to do. But if I were you, I would forgive me and feel sorry for me.

—Lucy McGee

I wrote the rest and then I went up to my closet and cried. That was my Saturday.

On Sunday, a black cloud was hanging over the McGee house. Seriously. The rain hadn't stopped. That wasn't all. Guess who else woke up sick? Leo and my mom. Everybody was in a worse mood than yesterday.

After a quiet breakfast, my dad drove me around in the rain, and I had to deliver my apology letters to each house. If I had a drone, I could have had *it* deliver my letters. That would have been a lot less embarrassing.

When I got back, Leo met me at the door. "Play worms with me, Lucy," he said.

"Forget it," I said.

"Lucy, please don't snap at your brother just because you're unhappy," my dad said.

"I'm unhappy, too," Leo said. "I'm sick, and Mom won't play with me."

My mom was trying to take a nap on the couch with Lily crawling all over her.

I put all my books from the bookshelf in a square on the floor and I sat inside it. "No one

is allowed to touch these books or talk to me," I said.

My mom gave my dad a look. "I hope Lucy knows she's going to have to put all those books back on the shelf."

Just then the rain started pounding down harder. Leo looked out the window and freaked out. "It's raining too much! The worms are drowning."

"Stop it, Leo!" I snapped. "I'm sick of worms."

"Lucy, that is not helpful." My mom picked up the remote and turned on Channel Four.

"Let's look at the weather report and see when they predict the rain will stop."

On TV, Janet Tandy, Scarlett's mom, was standing in front of a big map, talking about the weather. "Rain through midnight tonight. Tomorrow and Tuesday should be sunny and clear. Wednesday, some clouds and cooler temperatures will come in from the northwest. And we'll have a special surprise—a group of students from Slido Creek Elementary will be here. They've written songs about the weather, and we'll be rolling out the first one on Wednesday. Join us!"

My heart sank.

"Rain through midnight!" Leo
cried. "That's too much rain for the
worms!"

"My life is over!" I yelled at Leo. "Who cares
about worms?"

"You are mean, Lucy!" Leo grabbed one of
my books and threw it at me.

"Leo!" my mom yelled, and Leo started
crying.

I stomped upstairs and slammed my bedroom door. "I'm never coming out!" I yelled.

Chapter Nineteen

NO BLUES SNOOZE

We have a McGee rule. Chase away the blues before you snooze. It means you can't go to bed mad.

So after a while, I heard footsteps. And then a knock on my closet door. And then the door opened.

My mom was holding Lily and my dad was holding Leo.

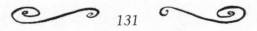

Everybody looked horrible. Everybody's hair was messy and everybody's nose was red and runny.

"Time for a talk," my mom said, and they all sat on my bed.

That bed looked nice with everybody all cozy on it, but I stayed in the closet.

"Leo has something to say," my mom said.

"I'm sorry for throwing a book at your head, Lucy," Leo said.

Sometimes people say they're sorry and they don't really mean it. When someone says they're sorry and they really mean it, your heart kind of gets a squeeze. Leo squeezed my heart.

"I'm sorry for yelling at you, Leo," I said.

"You yelled so loud you hurt my ears, Lucy," Leo said.

My parents laughed because Leo yells way

louder than me. And I sort of laughed and then I started crying and then I ran out of the closet and climbed on the bed. "I'm really sorry for everything." They hugged me, and my feelings started pouring out. "I love writing songs and singing so much. I get too excited and—"

Just then, our front doorbell rang.

"Who could that be?" my mom asked.

They left Leo and Lily with me and went down to answer the door.

Leo looked at me with big eyes. "Do you think it's the police?" he asked.

"Why would it be the police?" I asked, wiping my eyes.

"Because we were both really bad," he said.

Lily crawled into my lap and tried to give me her pacifier.

"Come on, let's find out who it is," I said.

Leo, Lily, and I crept to the top of the stairs. I heard a familiar voice. It was Scarlett's dad. I couldn't hear what he was saying. After a few minutes, he left, and we raced back to my room.

"Well, that was interesting," my mom said.

"Take a look at this," my dad said, and handed me a piece of paper.

Dear Songwriting Club,

I, Phillip Lee, believe that we should NOT sing on TV unless Lucy can sing with us. Even though Lucy made some mistakes, she is an excellent songwriter. I mean, come on, people! She wrote most of the songs we're singing.

If you agree, please sign below. If Lucy's parents see this, then maybe they'll let her sing.

Signed,

Phillip Lee (remember it was my idea to start the Songwriting Club)

Phillip Lee

Resa

Pab.

Nathalie

Scarlett

SAKI

mara

Victoria

"Phillip is one great friend," my mom said.

I wanted to agree, but I had a lump in my throat.

My dad explained. "Scarlett's dad said that Phillip went to Scarlett's house with the letter and asked Scarlett to sign it. Then Scarlett showed it to her dad and mom."

"Everybody is hoping we'll let you go to the TV studio on Wednesday," my mom said. "Janet wants to have the club do one song live and then record the rest of your songs so that Channel Four can air them throughout the month."

"Can I?" I asked.

"We're going to think about it," my parents said.

I jumped up and raced out the door.

"Where are you going?" my mom asked.

"I'm going to help you think!"

I ran downstairs. I started to put my books

back in the bookshelf. And then I noticed tissues on the floor. I put those in the trash even though they were disgusting. And then I noticed that the plants needed watering. I filled up the water pitcher. And then I noticed that there were dirty dishes in the sink, so I started washing them, and then I noticed that Lily's socks were on the floor, so I picked them up, and then my mom came in and stopped me.

"Lucy, what are you doing?"

"I'm being good so you'll let me go," I said.

"You're putting Lily's socks in the dishwasher!" she said.

I looked down and said, "Oops." And then we both started laughing.

"Your dad and I talked

137

it over," she said. "Singing on TV is a special thing. Since you apologized to everyone and you cleaned up after the party, we're going to let you go on Wednesday. But we'll expect you home right after school every other day this week and we'll expect extra-good behavior from you."

I jumped up and down and then I hugged her. "Thank you. Thank you."

She took my face in her hands. "You know who you should thank?"

I knew. The best friend a friend could be. My best friend . . . Phillip Lee.

Chapter Twenty

MCGEE TO LEE

Dear Phillip,

I once saw a huge store with nothing in it but candy. The letter you wrote was even better than that. Thanks!

Your friend,

Lucy McGee

Chapter Twenty-One

TV SHOW? LET'S GO!

On Monday and Tuesday, everybody at school was talking about how we were going to be on TV.

Lucy McGee! A star on TV!

Then Wednesday came! The sky was full of dark cumulonimbus clouds and the winds were whipping through the trees. All morning, it stayed the same way.

During recess, we worked on a thunderstorm song and practiced it. At the end, a bunch of first graders came over to us and told us they were going to watch and asked for our autographs.

Finally school was over. We got our ukes and ran to meet our parents in the parking lot. Victoria's mom, Scarlett's babysitter, and my dad were the car pool drivers.

Phillip, Resa, and I got into our minivan. Lily and Leo were both there, of course. As we rode, we sang all our songs. Lily clapped and tried to sing along, but Leo wouldn't smile.

While my dad talked to Phillip and Resa, Leo turned to me. "I want to be in your club. I want to be on TV," he whispered.

"You can't, Leo. But Dad is taking you and Lily to the bagel shop and you can watch us on Dad's laptop." We passed the bagel shop, and I pointed. "See? That'll be fun."

After two blocks, we passed a playground near a pond. "If I can't be on TV, I want to go there and play with worms." Leo pointed at the park.

"A big storm is coming," I said. "You have to stay inside."

I looked out the window. The sky had turned green and the clouds looked like they were

going to burst. We couldn't have a more exciting weather day!

Scarlett's mom met us in the lobby with her assistant, Tom. Then she had to go get a weather update. "This storm is moving fast!" she said.

Tom took us down a long hall to the main studio. There wasn't just one studio, there were lots of different rooms with stuff inside. One small room had a bunch of video screens showing views from different

143

cameras at the same time. "We have a new set of weather drones," Tom said. "We send them out to capture videos of severe weather."

"Drones!" Phillip and I looked at each other. So cool.

First we went to the main studio for a real rehearsal. It wasn't anything like the TV studio in our media center. This was big with huge lights, five different cameras, a main news desk in the middle, and a weather desk with a big computer and a green screen on the right.

Tom gave us each a place to stand in front of the green screen. He put Pablo in the center with Scarlett because they were the tallest. Nobody argued. He gave us tips for performing and we sang our song twice, pretending that the cameras were rolling.

"Great job," Tom said. "Don't move. I need to speak with Janet."

"I can't believe it," Phillip whispered.

"Believe what?" I whispered back.

"We're all getting along perfectly."

It was true. We looked around. Everybody in the Songwriting Club was smiling.

"When we get famous and move to Hollywood," Resa whispered, "let's all buy a house with a swimming pool and live in it together."

"One for all and all for the Songwriting Club!" I whispered.

We all gave each other a thumbs-up.

It was really happening—we were going to be on TV!

A voice came from the booth. "Places. Three minutes, people."

The anchorman and anchorwoman sat at the news desk, fixing their hair and microphones. Mrs. Tandy sat at the weather desk in front of the computer.

Tom adjusted his headset and stood behind the camera operators. "Okay, kids. Nobody move. After the anchors finish the news update, Janet will introduce you, then I'll point to you, and you look at this camera and sing your song. When you're done, don't move or talk until we give you the cue that it's okay. Then I'll take you to another studio and we'll tape the other songs." He smiled. "That will be more relaxed and fun."

"Showtime!" Phillip whispered.

We were smiling and ready.

"Hold on!" Mrs. Tandy worked at her computer. "Breaking news—a tornado was just spotted in Elkton! Hail and winds likely at seventy miles per hour." She turned to us. "Sorry, kids, you can't sing your song. We need to tell everyone to seek shelter immediately."

A voice came from a booth. "Adjusting the teleprompter. Ebony, you'll lead with it."

The anchorwoman nodded.

"Sixty seconds."

"We could do a tornado song!" Scarlett said.

"No," Mrs. Tandy said. "If we have kids singing, people might not take it seriously. This is an emergency."

"But Mom—" Scarlett started to whine.

Mrs. Tandy said to Tom, "Clear the kids! Quick!"

Our dream was squashed!

As Tom rushed us to the door, I thought I couldn't feel worse. But then Mrs. Tandy called out, "There's more breaking news! Wait, Lucy!"

I turned around. She had her cell phone out and a terrible look on her face.

"Lucy," she said. "Your dad is texting. Leo is missing!"

Chapter Twenty-Two

DANGEROUS
FORECAST?
MUST THINK FAST!

My heart was beating like crazy.

"Janet? What's going on?" the voice from the booth said. "We're on in thirty seconds."

"It's my neighbor Moz McGee," Mrs. Tandy said. "He can't find Leo, his son. Leo must have walked out of the shop they were in. Moz has looked everywhere. He just called the police for help." She looked at me again. "Lucy, he wants to know if you have any idea where Leo might be."

"Fifteen seconds, everyone," the voice from the booth said. "We have to roll. We'll confirm with the police and make an announcement about the missing child at the next update."

Tom was holding the studio door open. Half my friends were in and half were out. All of them were staring at me. My mind was swirling around like a tornado! I pictured poor little Leo out in the storm. What if he got hurt? What if we couldn't find him? He would be so scared.

"Ten seconds."

Then a thought popped into my head. "I might know where he is!" I said.

"Tell Tom!" Mrs. Tandy said, and we hustled out the door as the cameras switched on and the anchorwoman began to talk.

Out in the hallway, Tom looked at me.

"I think he might have gone to a park that we passed on our way," I said. "It's not far from here. Can we send a weather drone to look?"

Tom's eyes popped open. "Great idea!"

We ran toward the drone control room. Tom told my friends to wait in the hallway outside and took me in.

"Leo will be okay!" Phillip called out.

It was a nice thing for him to say, but my whole body felt shaky.

Tom talked to the woman in charge of programming the drones and then he gave me his phone and told me to call my dad and tell him what we were doing.

"Oh, Lucy, we have to find him," my dad said. Then his voice got as shaky as I felt. He stopped talking.

Tom took the phone. "We'll keep you on the line so you can hear what's happening, Mr. McGee. Just hold on." He turned on the cell phone's speaker and handed it back to me.

"Which park?" the drone woman asked.

"I don't know the name, but it has a big pond and we passed it on the way here."

"Adler Park!" the woman said. "No problem. We have a drone and a truck not too far away. Tom, let's get a news crew ready just in case."

"Dad," I said into the phone. "I think he went to a park near the bagel shop called Adler."

"I'm going!" he said. "Victoria's mom came here. She can watch Lily."

"No, Dad! There's a tornado coming. You can't go outside!" He didn't answer. "Dad? Dad?"

Things started happening all at once.

While Tom arranged on his phone for a news crew to head to Adler Park, the woman programmed the drone to fly there, too.

"Here's the live video feed," she told me, and nodded at the big screen in front of us.

"Dad," I said. "We're sending a drone to look for Leo. We're watching it now."

"I'm almost at the park," my dad said. "What do you see?"

"The treetops are blowing like mad, and the sky is green. The wind is shaking the drone!" My stomach got a bad feeling. It was a big park with a pond and a basketball court and no sign of my brother.

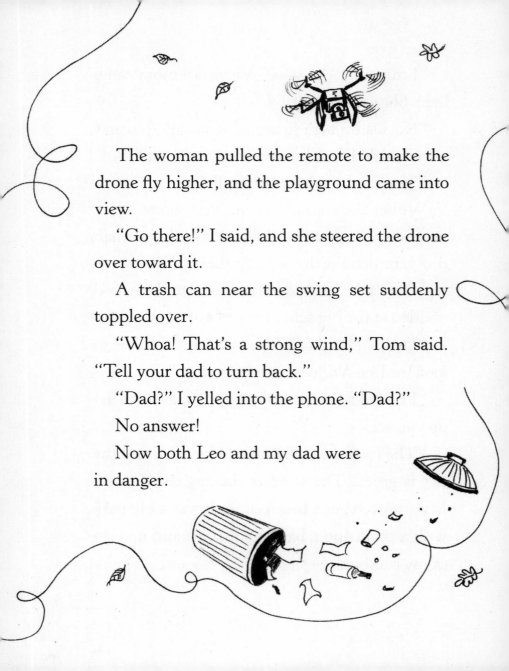

The woman pulled the remote to make the drone fly higher, and the playground came into view.

"Go there!" I said, and she steered the drone over toward it.

A trash can near the swing set suddenly toppled over.

"Whoa! That's a strong wind," Tom said. "Tell your dad to turn back."

"Dad?" I yelled into the phone. "Dad?"

No answer!

Now both Leo and my dad were in danger.

Chapter Twenty-Three

WHERE CAN YOU BE, OH LEO?

"Dad?" I pressed the phone to my ear. "Are you there?"

All I could hear was wind, and then my dad's voice came. "I'm trying to find the playground now, Lucy."

The drone flew toward a pirate ship on the playground where there were climbing ropes and a slide. The ropes were whipping against the sides of the ship.

"Nobody's here," Tom said. "Let's check by the picnic area."

"Wait!" I said. "Leo likes worms. I could imagine him crawling under that slide to be near the worms. Can you look under that?"

The drone flew over the top of the ship and started lowering. A shape came into view but then the drone was knocked away by the wind.

"Go back! I saw something!" I said, and the drone operator tried again.

The drone turned and dipped down under the slide, and Leo's surprised face popped into view!

"That's him!" I yelled. "Dad! He's under the slide!"

"We've located the boy!" Tom said to the news crew. "Head to the pirate ship on the playground!" Then he called the director. "We've got a rescue. We need to go live on this."

The drone flew up, and we could see the news van pulling up from one side and my dad running toward the pirate ship from the other side.

"There's my dad!" I said, and pointed.

The news crew hopped out of the van with their cameras rolling.

"Leo!" my dad called out.

Leo crawled out from under the slide and ran toward my dad. The wind was whipping so hard,

Leo was blown backward instead of forward. My dad ran and scooped him up in his arms. Leo squeezed tight and buried his face in my dad's neck, looking just like a little koala bear.

There was a huge cheer, and I turned around. The door was open slightly and all my friends were in the hallway clapping.

I turned back to look at the video screen. The news crew was leading my dad back to the van, videoing the whole way. Holding Leo, my dad climbed into the back-seat. The look on his face got me. My dad was gulping for breath and tears were streaming down his cheeks. He looked so hap-py to have Leo in his arms again that I started to cry. Then Leo finally let go and turned and the camera got

a close-up of his face. A big, wet, goofy smile.
Even though I was still crying, I laughed, too.

When you love your family, you just want
them to be safe. And the emotions you feel are
so big, they have to come out.

Tom gave me a tissue. "Good job, Lucy," he
said.

When we walked out, all my friends hugged
me and patted me on the back, and I almost
started crying again.

Tom stopped and listened to his headset. "Lucy, they want to run the rescue footage. Can you do a quick live interview?"

I nodded, and the next thing I knew I was sitting at the news desk next to the anchorwoman!

Chapter Twenty-Four

LUCY MCGEE ON TV!

"Lucy McGee, we hear it was your idea to use one of the Channel Four weather drones to find your brother. How did you think of that?"

The camera turned to me. I blinked. "The idea just popped into my brain. My brother told me he wanted to play in that park with the worms. So

I figured that was where he'd go. He loves worms."

The anchorwoman smiled. "I'm sure your family will be very proud of you. Can you tell our viewing audience why you're here today?"

I looked over at the Songwriting Club. Tom let them stand by the doorway as long as they didn't make a sound.

"I'm here with my friends. We have a songwriting club, and we've been singing about the weather together."

The anchorwoman looked into the camera. "That's right. Lucy McGee and our young guests from Slido Creek Elementary's Songwriting Club were going to sing live today, but the storm interrupted. We'll record their songs and bring them to you throughout the month."

I smiled. I'd forgotten that we were still going to make the recordings.

"Stay tuned to Channel Four," the anchorwoman said.

"For weather updates, news, and more!" I said.

She looked at me and smiled. "Lucy McGee knows how to rhyme."

I shrugged. "I make rhymes all the time!"

Chapter Twenty-Five

TONS OF FUN

The storm passed and nobody was hurt. After that, we had fun. Tom took us to another room, where we recorded our weather songs. He said they'll run our songs when it's "appropriate." Like, they'll show the sunny-weather song when it's sunny and the rainy-weather song when it's raining.

Our parents came to pick us up, and when I saw Leo and Lily and my dad, we gave each other huge hugs.

My dad had bought bagels, so we made pizza bagels for dinner. Yum.

"You were a star, Lucy," my mom said as we were finishing dinner. "We're proud of your quick thinking."

"I was a star, too," Leo said. "I was on TV, too."

"Me too," Lily said, even though she wasn't.

"Leo," my dad said. "Getting on TV because you were in danger is not the good kind of star to be. Never leave Mom or me again, right?"

Leo nodded. "I won't." And then a funny look came over his face and a little shiver went through his body. "I was scared."

"We were all scared, Leo," my mom said, and hugged him. "That was a big storm."

I took my last pizza-bagel bite. "I can't wait to see one of our recordings on TV."

My dad fist-bumped me. "We're going to have to watch the weather on Channel Four all month. Go, Songwriting Club!"

"Can I be in your club, Lucy?" Leo asked.

I looked at my mom and dad. It was kind of awkward. I mean, I love Leo, but he's just too little to be in my club.

"You can start a club of your own," my dad said. He's a quick thinker, too.

"No, I can't," Leo said. "I don't know how to make a club."

"Pick something you like to do," I said. "And then invite people to come to your club and do it with you."

Leo jumped up with a big grin. "I like to play worms! I'm making a Worm Club! Will you be in it?"

"Sure," my dad said.

"I'm in," my mom said.

"Me too," Lily said.

Leo ran into the living room and started wriggling on the carpet. "Come on!"

We joined him and wiggled and wriggled and giggled together. Tons of fun!

That night, as I was getting ready for bed, I felt a song inside me. I picked up my uke and my songwriting notebook and crawled into bed. Through my window, I could see the moon and stars.

I played around with an idea. I wrote a draft and changed the words until I liked it. Then I picked up my uke and sang.

When the wind has gone to sleep
and the moon above is smiling,
I can curl up in my bed
and feel the love that's lighting
up the inside of my heart
even when it's dark
outside.

Come and sing with me.
We'll be so safe and warm.
Hold each other tight
through every scary storm.
Come and sing with me
tonight.

There was a huge
cheer, and I turned
to the door. It was open
slightly and my mom and
dad and Leo and Lily were in
the hallway clapping.

There was a huge cheer, and I turned to the door. It was open slightly and my mom and dad and Leo and Lily were in the hallway clapping.

I laughed. "A new song from me, Lucy McGee!"

THE SONGWRITING CLUB SONGS

Have fun with the songs in this book. You can hear the songs and sing along by going to the special Lucy page on my site: www.maryamato.com/lucy-songs.

You can also find out more about making up your own songs and learning how to play songs on a ukulele, piano, or guitar.

THE RAIN SONG

It drizzled all night
and it's pouring right now.
You think it's raining cats and dogs?
I'd say it's raining . . . cows!

Before you leave the house,
pack an extra pair of socks,
especially if you have to walk
a couple of blocks.

The puddles are so deep
they're probably filled with fish.
When you step in a puddle
your shoes go squish.

So pack that extra pair
of socks for your feet.
Your toes will thank you
and think you're sweet.

NO ONE CAN HEAR ME

Rain laughs against the glass.
The clock is ticking loud and fast.
My pencil shouts across this page
while other voices drown me out.

No one can hear me.
No one can hear me.
No one can hear me now.

Why can't I evaporate and rise up
from the ground,
    become a cloud and float to Idaho
    and let my rain come thundering
down?
    Then at least someone in Idaho
would hear me falling down.

Hear me falling
Hear me falling
Hear me falling down.

THE FOG SONG

Life today turned upside down.
Clouds are drooping to the ground.
The sun got scared and stayed in bed.
Are those trees or ghosts ahead?
Grayish mists are deeply creeping.
Is the whole world wet and weeping?
Wolves and zombies—did I mention?—
love this weather. Pay attention!
As you walk alone, beware!
The fog can hide what's lurking there.

THE GOOD NIGHT SONG

When the wind has gone to sleep
and the moon above is smiling,
I can curl up in my bed
and feel the love that's lighting
up the inside of my heart
even when it's dark
outside.

Come and sing with me.
We'll be so safe and warm.
Hold each other tight
through every scary storm.
Come and sing with me
tonight.

SING ALONG WITH MORE LUCY MCGEE ADVENTURES!